The Bear
That Wasn't

FRANK TASHLIN

DOVER PUBLICATIONS, INC.
New York

Published in Canada by General Publishing Company, Ltd., 30 Lesmill Road, Don Mills, Toronto, Ontario.
Published in the United Kingdom by Constable and Company, Ltd., 3 The Lanchesters, 162–164 Fulham Palace Road, London W6 9ER.

Bibliographical Note

This Dover Children's Thrift Classic edition, first published in 1995, is a slightly altered republication of the Dover edition published in 1962. The work was originally published by E. P. Dutton & Co., Inc., in 1946.

Library of Congress Cataloging-in-Publication Data

Tashlin, Frank.
    The bear that wasn't / Frank Tashlin.
      p.   cm. — (Dover children's thrift classics)
    Summary: After hibernating for the winter, a bear wakes up to discover that a huge factory has been built over his cave and that nobody believes he is a bear.
    ISBN 0-486-28787-4 (pbk.)
    [1. Bears—Fiction. 2. Identity—Fiction.] I. Title. II. Series.
PZ7.T21114Be   1995
[Fic]—dc20   95-17846
                                                      CIP
                                                        AC

Manufactured in the United States of America
Dover Publications, Inc., 31 East 2nd Street, Mineola, N.Y. 11501

FOR

MY SON

CHRISTOPHER

KERRY

Once upon a time, in fact it was on a Tuesday, the Bear stood at the edge of a great forest and gazed up at the sky. Away up high, he saw a flock of geese flying south.

Then he gazed up at the trees of the forest. The leaves
had turned all yellow and brown and were falling
from the branches.

He knew when the geese flew south and the leaves fell
from the trees, that winter would soon be here and snow
would cover the forest. It was time to go into a cave
and hibernate.

And that was just what he did.

Not long afterward, in fact it was on a Wednesday, men came ... lots of men, with charts and maps and surveying instruments. They charted and mapped and surveyed all over the place.

Then more men came, lots of men with steamshovels and
saws and tractors and axes. They steamshoveled and
sawed and tractored and **axed** all over the place.

They worked, **and** worked, and worked, **and** finally they
built a great, big, huge,

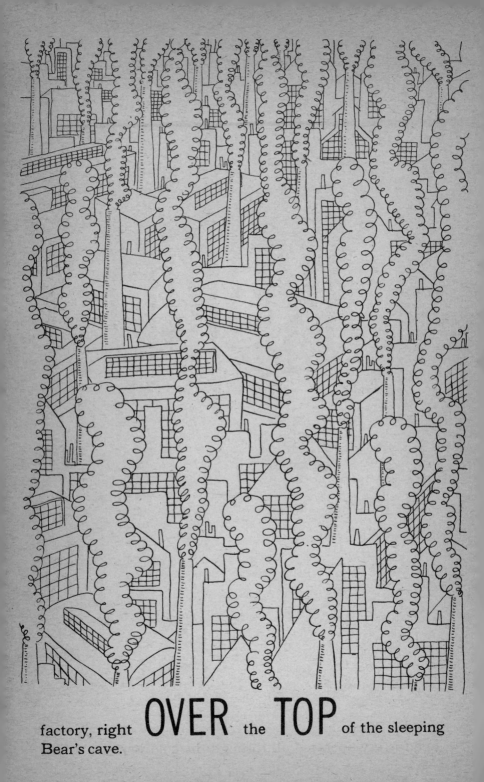

factory, right **OVER** the **TOP** of the sleeping
Bear's cave.

The factory operated all through the cold winter.

And
then
it
was
SPRING
again

Deep down under one of the factory
buildings the Bear awoke. He
blinked his eyes and yawned.

Then he stood up sleepily and
looked around. It was very dark.
He could hardly see.

Then he saw a light in the distance.
"Oh, there's the entrance to the cave,"
he said, and yawned again.

He walked up the stairs to the entrance

and stepped out into the bright spring sunshine. His eyes were only half opened, as he was still very sleepy.

His eyes didn't stay half opened long.

They suddenly POPPED wide apart.
He looked straight ahead.

Where was the forest?
Where was the grass?
Where were the trees?
Where were the flowers?

WHAT HAD HAPPENED?

Where was he?

Things looked so strange. He didn't know where he was.

But we do, don't we? We know that he was right in the
middle of the busy factory.

"I must be dreaming," he said.
"Of course that's it, I'm dreaming."
So he closed his eyes and
pinched himself.
Then he opened his eyes very
slowly and looked about. The big
buildings were still there. It wasn't
a dream. It was real.

Just then a man came out of a door.

"Hey, you get back to work," the man said. "I'm the *Foreman* and I'll report you for not working."

The Bear said, "I don't work here. I'm a Bear."

The Foreman laughed very loud.

"That's a fine excuse for a man to keep from doing any work."

"Saying he's a Bear."

The Bear said, "But, I am a Bear."

The Foreman stopped laughing. He was very mad.

"Don't try to fool me," he said. "You're not a Bear. You're a silly man who needs a shave and wears a fur coat. I'm going to take you to the *General Manager*."

The Bear said, "No, you're mistaken. I am a Bear."

The General Manager was very mad, too.

He said, "You're not a Bear. You're a silly man who needs a shave and wears a fur coat. I'm going to take you to the *Third* Vice President."

The Bear said, "I'm sorry to hear you say that ... You see, I am a Bear."

The Third Vice President was even madder.

He got up out of his chair and said, "You're not a Bear. You're a silly man who needs a shave and wears a fur coat. I'm going to take you to the *Second* Vice President."

The Bear leaned over his desk and said, "But that isn't true. I am a Bear, just a plain, ordinary, everyday Bear."

The Second Vice President was more than mad or madder. He was furious.

He pointed his finger at the Bear and said, "You're not a Bear. You're a silly man who needs a shave and wears a fur coat. I'm going to take you to the *First* Vice President."

"Who? Me?" the Bear asked. "How can you say that, when I am a Bear?"

The First Vice President yelled in rage.

He said, "You're not a Bear. You're a silly man who needs a shave and wears a fur coat. I'm going to take you to the *President*."

The Bear pleaded, "This is a dreadful error, you know, because ever since I can remember, I've always been a Bear."

"Listen," the Bear told the President, "I don't work here.
I'm a Bear, and please don't say I'm a silly man who needs
a shave and wears a fur coat, because the
First Vice President and the Second Vice President
and the Third Vice President and the General Manager

and the Foreman, have told me that already."

"Thank you for telling me," the President said. "I won't say it, but that's just what I think you are."

The Bear said, "I'm a Bear."

The President smiled and said, "You can't be a Bear. Bears are only in a zoo or a circus. They're never inside a factory and that's where you are; inside a factory. So how can you be a Bear?"

The Bear said, "But I am a Bear."

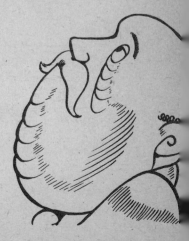

The President said, "Not only are you a silly man who needs a shave and wears a fur coat, but you are also very stubborn. So I'm going to **prove** it to you, once and for all, that you are *not* a Bear."

The Bear said, "But I *am a* Bear."

AND

SO

THEY

ALL

GOT

INTO

THE

PRESIDENT'S

CAR

AND

DROVE

TO

THE

ZOO

"Is he a *Bear*?" the President asked the zoo Bears.

The zoo Bears said, "No, he isn't a Bear, because if he were a Bear, he wouldn't be outside the cage with you. He would be inside the cage with us."

The Bear said, "But I am a Bear."

A little baby zoo Bear said, "I know what he is. He's a silly man who needs a shave and wears a fur coat."

All the zoo Bears laughed.

The Bear said, "But I am a Bear."

AND
SO
THEY
ALL
LEFT
THE
ZOO
AND
DROVE
SIX
HUNDRED
MILES
AWAY
TO
THE
NEAREST
CIRCUS

"Is he a *Bear?*" the President asked the circus Bears.
The circus Bears said, "No, he isn't a Bear, because if he
were a Bear, he wouldn't be sitting in a grandstand seat
with you. He would be wearing a little hat with a striped
ribbon on it, holding on to a balloon and riding a bicycle
with us."　　　　　　The Bear said, "But I am a Bear."

One little baby circus Bear said, "I know what he is. He's a silly man who needs a shave and wears a fur coat."

All the circus Bears almost fell off their bicycles laughing.

The Bear said, "But I am a Bear."

They left the circus and drove
back to the factory.

And so they put the Bear to work on a big machine with a lot of other men. The Bear worked on the big machine for many, many months.

One day a long time afterward, the factory closed down
and all the workers left and went home.
The Bear walked along far behind them. He was all
alone, and had no place to go.

As he walked along,
he happened to gaze up
at the sky. Away up high,
he saw a flock of geese flying
south.

Then the Bear gazed up at the trees. The leaves had turned
all yellow and brown and were falling from the branches.

The Bear knew when the geese flew south and the leaves fell from the trees, that winter would soon be here and snow would cover the forest. It was time to go into a cave and hibernate.

So he walked over to a huge tree that had a cave hollowed out beneath its roots. He was just about to go into it, when he stopped and said,

"But I **CAN'T** go into a cave and hibernate.
I'm **NOT** a Bear. I'm a silly man who needs a shave
and wears a fur coat."

So winter came. The snow fell. It covered the forest and it covered him. He sat there, shivering with cold and he said, "But I sure wish I was a Bear."

The longer he sat there the colder he became. His toes were freezing, his ears were freezing and his teeth were chattering. Icicles covered his nose and chin. He had been told so often, that he was a silly man who needed a shave and wore a fur coat, that he felt it must be true.

So he just sat there, because he didn't know what a silly man who needed a shave and wore a fur coat would do, if he were freezing to death in the snow. The poor Bear was very lonely and very sad. He didn't know what to think.

Then suddenly he got up and
walked through the deep
snow toward the cave.

Inside, it was cosy and snug.
The icy wind and cold, cold
snow couldn't reach him here.
He felt warm all over.

He sank down on a bed of pine boughs and soon he was happily asleep and dreaming sweet dreams, just like all bears do, when they hibernate.
So even though the

FOREMAN and the *GENERAL MANAGER* and the *THIRD VICE-PRESIDENT* and the *SECOND VICE-PRESIDENT* and the	*FIRST* *VICE-PRESIDENT* and the *PRESIDENT* and the *ZOO BEARS* and the *CIRCUS BEARS*

had said, he was a silly man who needed a shave and wore a fur coat, I don't think he really believed it, do you? No, indeed, he knew he wasn't a silly man,

and he wasn't a silly Bear either.